REAL MADRID CF

by Todd Kortemeier

EUROPE'S BEST SOCCER CLUBS

SportsZone

An Imprint of Abdo Publishing
abdopublishing.com

abdopublishing.com

Published by Abdo Publishing, a division of ABDO, PO Box 398166, Minneapolis, Minnesota 55439.

Printed in the United States of America, North Mankato, Minnesota
062017
092017

THIS BOOK CONTAINS RECYCLED MATERIALS

Cover Photos: Marcio Jose Sanchez/AP Images, foreground; AP Images, background
Interior Photos: Javier Garcia/Rex Features/AP Images, 4; Friso Gentsch/picture-alliance/dpa/AP Images, 9; Manu Fernandez/AP Images, 10, 12, 40; Laurence Griffiths/Getty Images Sport/Getty Images, 11; Staff/AFP/Getty Images, 14, 16; AP Images, 19; PA Wire/URN:15773215/AP Images, 20; Dean Bertoncelj/Shutterstock Images, 22; Juan R. Velasco/Shutterstock Images, 25; Marcos Mesa Sam Wordley/Shutterstock Images, 27; Paul Popper/Popperfoto/Getty Images, 28; Central Press/Hulton Archive/Getty Images, 31; Popperfoto/Getty Images, 33; Domenico Stinellis/AP Images, 35; Alastair Grant/AP Images, 36; Maxisport/AP Images, 38; Paul White/AP Images, 42

Editor: Patrick Donnelly
Series Designer: Craig Hinton
Content Consultant: Paul Logothetis, European soccer reporter

Publisher's Cataloging-in-Publication Data

Names: Kortemeier, Todd, author.
Title: Real Madrid CF / by Todd Kortemeier.
Description: Minneapolis, MN : Abdo Publishing, 2018. | Series: Europe's best soccer clubs | Includes bibliographical references and index.
Identifiers: LCCN 2016963099 | ISBN 9781532111365 (lib. bdg.) | ISBN 9781680789218 (ebook)
Subjects: LCSH: Soccer--Europe--History--Juvenile literature. | Soccer teams--Europe--History--Juvenile literature. | Soccer--Europe--Records--Juvenile literature. | Real Madrid Club de Fútbol (Soccer team)--Juvenile literature.
Classification: DDC 796.334--dc23
LC record available at http://lccn.loc.gov/2016963099

TABLE OF CONTENTS

Fly
Emirates

Gareth Bale was a key addition to the Real Madrid lineup in 2013.

CHAPTER 1

LA DÉCIMA

Real Madrid *Club de Fútbol* (CF) was sitting on top of the world in the summer of 2013. The club had a new manager in Carlo Ancelotti. It had signed world-class midfielder Gareth Bale. And the team known as *Los Blancos* had plenty of other top talent already in place. It had all the makings of a special season in the capital city of Spain.

With Bale, Luka Modrić, and Ángel Di María, Real featured a potent attack. Add in goal-scoring legend Cristiano Ronaldo and Real was able to give opponents fits. But in La Liga—Spain's top league—Real Madrid's two main rivals were ready with

EUROPEAN SOCCER

The European soccer season is broken down into different levels of competition. It can be confusing to keep track of it all. Here's a handy guide to help you follow the action.

League Play

The 20 best teams in Spain play in La Liga. Teams play all league opponents twice each season for 38 total games. The three teams with the worst records are relegated—or sent down—to the second division, which sends its top three teams up to replace them the next season.

European Play

The top three teams in La Liga qualify for the group stage of the Union of European Football Associations (UEFA) Champions League. This annual tournament involves the best teams from the top leagues throughout Europe. The Champions League debuted in 1992. It replaced the European Cup, a similar tournament that began in 1955.

The fourth place team enters Champions League play in the qualifying round. The next two teams from La Liga qualify for the UEFA Europa League. The Europa League is Europe's second-tier tournament. It runs in a similar manner to the Champions League but crowns its own winner. The Europa League debuted in 1971 as the UEFA Cup but was renamed in 2009.

Domestic Cups

Teams from the top four levels of Spanish soccer are eligible to play in the *Copa del Rey*, or King's Cup. Founded in 1903, the tournament is the oldest in Spain. The winning team automatically qualifies for the Europa League. It also faces the champion of La Liga in the *Supercopa de Espana* (Spanish Super Cup).

strong teams of their own. Neighbors Atlético Madrid pulled away to the 2013–14 league title. Barcelona finished second. It was a disappointing end to the season for Real.

But Los Blancos had a chance to make up for the disappointment with a strong showing in the Champions League. The club had once dominated that competition, but by 2013–14 it had been 13 seasons since its most recent title. And while Real struggled through its 2013–14 La Liga season, the team was rolling in the Champions League.

Ancelotti's team stormed through the group stage undefeated, scoring 20 goals and allowing only five. Ronaldo scored seven goals in Real's first three matches. Real easily moved on to the round of 16.

FAST FACT

Real Madrid won another major trophy in 2013–14. It beat rival Barcelona 2–1 in the final of the Copa del Rey.

Win or Go Home

In the knockout stage, Real crushed Schalke of Germany's Bundesliga by a two-game total score of 9–2. Ronaldo scored four of the goals. Another German foe, Borussia Dortmund, was up next. In the first game, Bale and Ronaldo scored in a 3–0 shutout. In the second leg, Real suffered its first loss of the tournament. But it was only by 2–0, meaning Real still won by a 3–2 total score.

Real faced yet another German squad, Bayern Munich, in the semifinals. Karim Benzema's goal held up as Real eked out a 1–0 win in the first leg. Los Blancos left no doubt in the second game, routing Bayern 4–0. Two Ronaldo goals put the game out of reach. It was on to the final in nearby Lisbon, Portugal.

The road between Madrid and Lisbon was busy that week. That's because not only had Real Madrid qualified but so had Atlético Madrid. The rivals had played each other more than 200 times, with Real usually coming out on top. But Atlético was a team on the rise and would put up a fight.

Rivals Rumble

Real looked to be up to the task early, dominating possession and creating scoring chances. But Atlético struck first. Diego Godín's header in the 36th minute sent Real into halftime trailing 1–0.

Real's supporters rallied the team in the second half. Los Blancos continued

Cristiano Ronaldo came up big in the Champions League knockout rounds.

Fly
Emirates

Goalkeeper Iker Casillas, *right*, couldn't stop Atlético from taking a lead in the first half.

to generate chances. Ancelotti brought on two substitutes to help the attack. But nothing seemed to work. Shots sailed inches wide. Free kicks were blocked in front.

Sergio Ramos, *4*, heads home the game-tying goal late in stoppage time.

At the 90-minute mark, the referee added five minutes of stoppage time. It was Real's last chance. With time running out, Real earned a corner kick. Modrić crossed the ball into the box. Real defender Sergio Ramos emerged from the crowd. With his head, he drove the ball to the far corner of the net, just under the goalkeeper's diving reach. Just like that, Real had new life.

Champions, Again

The game headed to extra time—two 15-minute periods. The first 15 minutes were scoreless. But the next 15 minutes would go down in Real Madrid history.

adidas
FINAL LISBON 2014
Fly
Emirates

Real took the lead in the 110th minute. Di María beat three defenders at the corner of the penalty box to drill a shot on goal. A rebound floated to the far post, and Bale headed it home. But Real kept attacking. Six minutes later, Marcelo—one of Ancelotti's subs—scored to put Real ahead by two. Then Ronaldo sealed it with a penalty kick. It was his record 17th goal of the tournament. Nearly dead after 90 minutes, Real blew past Atlético to win the title 4–1.

The victory was Real Madrid's 10th in a tournament that dated back to 1955–56. No other team had won that many. The feat was known as *La Décima* or "The Tenth." The players celebrated in shirts bearing the phrase.

The win also ushered in a new era of dominance for Real Madrid. In 2016 and 2017 Ronaldo and Bale teamed up again to lead Madrid to back-to-back Champions League victories. Real was the first team in the Champions League era to win consecutive titles. But its fans will always look back at La Décima as a landmark accomplishment for one of the top soccer clubs in the world.

Bale celebrates his go-ahead goal that gave Real Madrid its 10th European cup.

Alfredo Di Stefano led Real Madrid to the first five European Cup titles.

CHAPTER 2

A ROYAL CLUB

One day in 1900, a handful of soccer players jogged onto a field in Madrid, Spain. They played in t-shirts and rolled-up long pants. One of them was Julián Palacios. He loved the game, but it wasn't popular yet in Spain. He started Madrid Football Club in 1900 to have a place to play with his friends. He couldn't have known at the time that it would become one of the world's greatest teams.

Palacios was the club's first president. He also was its first captain. In March 1902 he gave control of the club to Juan Padros, who oversaw the club's growth into a professional

GA
QUALITE

soccer team. The club's board of directors organized the country's first soccer tournament. The Copa del Rey has since become an annual tournament. Madrid won four of the first six. During this time, the club did not play in a formal league. Aside from the Copa, Madrid played a few games each year against other teams from the same region.

Royal Honor

Madrid added another Copa in 1917, its first since 1908. In 1920 the club got an even bigger honor. The king of Spain, who was a big soccer fan, allowed the club to add the word *Real* (pronounced ray-ALL) to its name. *Real* means "royal" in Spanish. It reflected the club's special status as one of the king's favorite clubs. A crown was also added to the club's crest to reflect its new, lofty status.

La Liga played its first season in 1928–29. Real was the runner-up in the league and the Copa del Rey that season. To help put the team over the top, it signed the best goalkeeper in the world. Ricardo Zamora arrived in Madrid in 1930. Zamora joined Ciriaco and Jacinto Quincoces to form the core

Goalkeeper Ricardo Zamora was the anchor of Real's defense in the early 1930s.

of Real's defense in the early 1930s. They had a dream season in 1931–32. Real went unbeaten in La Liga. With the trio together, Real won two La Liga titles and two Copas in four years.

Real was flying high. But tragedy soon struck the country. In 1936 Spain was plunged into civil war. The club had already lost the title "Real" when a new government took over in 1931. Known only as "Madrid CF," the royal crown was removed from its crest as well. Now its very existence was threatened by the war.

FAST FACT

Real Madrid is known as *Los Blancos*, which means "the whites" in Spanish. That's because they have always worn white jerseys and shorts at home. In 1925 they experimented with black shorts. But the team quickly went back to white.

Uncertain Times

La Liga suspended play for three years. Some players died in battle. Some fled the country and never returned. The war ended in 1939, and on April 19, what was left of the club had a meeting. Its stadium was destroyed, and few players remained. But they were determined to rebuild.

Madrid, like much of Spain, put soccer on hold as it was ravaged by the Spanish Civil War.

Real captain Miguel Munoz, *left*, shakes hands with Manchester United captain Roger Byrne before a 1957 European Cup match.

In 1943 Santiago Bernabéu became the new club president. By then the club had regained its crown and royal name. Under Bernabéu's guidance, Real Madrid also regained its status as the best team in Spain. It won back-to-back Copas in 1945 and 1946. And a new stadium opened in 1947. The stadium would one day be named for Bernabéu.

Real Madrid's golden era occurred right after a major change in European soccer. In 1955–56 a new tournament began to determine the best club team in Europe. Behind superstar striker Alfredo Di Stefano, Real won the first five European Cups.

The tournament continues today as the Champions League. No other team has won more than three in a row.

Real won another European Cup in 1966. The team continued to be competitive in La Liga after that. It has won at least three league titles in every decade since the 1950s. But it took more than 30 years for Real to win another European title. Defender Roberto Carlos and forward Raúl led Real past Italian team Juventus in the 1998 Champions League final. Then it won another European title in an all-Spanish final in 2000. With young goalie Iker Casillas in net, Real shut out Valencia 3–0.

A new group of stars nicknamed *Galacticos* led Madrid to another European title two years later. Zinedine Zidane, Luís Figo, and the rest helped restore Real Madrid's status as one of the best soccer teams in the world. They passed the baton to Cristiano Ronaldo and the next generation of Real stars, who continued the club's pursuit of excellence.

FAST FACT

Real Madrid City opened in 2005. It is the club's training facility and headquarters. The complex covers an area of 1.2 million square meters (12.9 million square feet). There is also a small stadium where Madrid's reserve team plays.

The crown atop the Real Madrid crest reflects its royal status.

CHAPTER 3

LOS BLANCOS

Real Madrid is one of the most valuable sports teams in the world. In 2016 it was valued at $3.7 billion by *Forbes* magazine. That was second only to the Dallas Cowboys among all sports teams.

Many top soccer clubs are owned by some of the world's richest people. Real Madrid's ownership is unusual. The club is owned by its fans. Members of the club buy shares in it and vote on a president to run it. Members don't make money off the club, which reinvests its profits back into the team. But they play a part in making it successful.

Fan ownership wouldn't work without dedicated support. And Real's fans are some of the best anywhere. The club averaged nearly 70,000 fans per game at the Bernabéu stadium in 2015–16. And the club's support extends well beyond the city of Madrid. Real claims to have the most official supporters clubs in the world—more than 2,200. Most are in Spain, but Switzerland has 13, and the United States and Morocco each have nine.

FAST FACT

Real Madrid and Bayern Munich of Germany have become huge Champions League rivals. They have played more matches against each other than any other two teams in that tournament. As two of the best teams in Europe, they are almost always in the competition.

Classic Rivals

When Real and Barcelona get together, it's always a massive event. The rivalry is known as *El Clasico*. It's the most important game of the year, and not just for Spanish soccer fans. More than 400 million people around the world tune in to watch each game. It easily tops the Super Bowl for worldwide viewers. That's no surprise for two of the most popular teams in the world. Both clubs are among the leaders in jersey sales, social media followers, and

The rivalry between Real and Barcelona both divides and unites Spanish soccer fans.

player salaries. And they have dominated Spanish soccer. Real won its 33rd La Liga championship in 2016–17. Barcelona was second with 24 titles.

The match carries political meaning, too. Barcelona is located in the Catalonia region of Spain. Some Catalonians wish to be a separate country from Spain. But Madrid is the capital of Spain. Supporters of Real Madrid are seen as also supporting a united Spain. These off-field tensions add to the rivalry.

While Real and Barcelona battle to rule Spain, Real and Atlético Madrid battle for Madrid. Though it's not as noteworthy as El Clasico, the teams have a long rivalry. Atlético was founded in 1923. Historically, Real was supported by rich fans. Atlético supporters were more from the working class. These divisions have faded over time. Now each club has all kinds of fans. Many great players have played for both clubs. Hugo Sánchez, one of Real's most famous players, got his start at Atlético. Real Madrid was undefeated in 25 straight league matches against Atlético from 1999 to 2013 and defeated Atlético in the Champions League final twice in three years, adding further fuel to the fire.

FAST FACT

Clubs that finish at the bottom of La Liga are relegated to play in a lower division. This has never happened to Real Madrid or Barcelona.

Estadio Santiago Bernabéu is a shining soccer palace in the heart of Madrid.

Estadio Santiago Bernabéu

Estadio Santiago Bernabéu opened in 1947. It has become one of Europe's most famous stadiums. With seating for more than 80,000, it's also one of the biggest. But it also has a bright future. In 2017 renovations began to add a retractable roof and attached hotel to the stadium. The $425 million dollar project will make the Bernabéu one of the most luxurious venues in the world.

Alfredo Di Stefano is swarmed by English schoolboys before a 1957 European Cup game in Manchester.

CHAPTER 4

PAST LEGENDS

One of Real Madrid's greatest players almost ended up in the hands of its fiercest rival. Alfredo Di Stefano was dominating South American soccer when Real and Barcelona came calling in 1953. Both clubs wanted the Argentina native to sign with them.

At first, each club signed him to a contract. The Spanish soccer association announced a compromise. The plan was for Di Stefano to switch off years playing for one or the other. He began playing with Real Madrid. But after he started slowly, Barcelona decided to sell its rights to him. Four days later,

Di Stefano showed what a big mistake that was by scoring three goals in a game against Barcelona. Di Stefano led Real to the league title in his first season in Spain, the club's first championship since before the Spanish Civil War. With Di Stefano leading the way, Real was back.

FAST FACT

Midfielder Francisco Gento played with Real from 1953 to 1971. He played on teams that won 23 trophies. No other Real player has won as much hardware.

All-Time Greats

In Di Stefano's 11 seasons, Real won La Liga eight times. It also won the first five European Cups. The fifth win came in 1960. Real played Eintracht Frankfurt from West Germany in the final before 125,000 fans at Hampden Park in Glasgow, Scotland. Di Stefano had a hat trick in the 7–3 Real win. The game is considered one of the greatest of all time.

Di Stefano scored 308 goals in 396 games with Real. He later coached the club and became its president. Near the end of his playing career, Ferenc Puskás joined the club.

Ferenc Puskás was already a legend when he left Hungary for Madrid in 1958.

The Hungarian was 31 years old in 1958, but he had plenty of life in his left foot. Puskás scored 242 goals for Real, leading La Liga in scoring four times. Starting in 1960–61, Real won five straight La Liga titles. When Puskás died in 2006, FIFA named its goal of the year award after him.

In midfield Real was anchored by José Martínez Sánchez, nicknamed Pirri. He could do it all. He could play a defensive or offensive role. Pirri could also score goals. He had 172 of them over a long career with Real. He played from 1964 to 1980 and won 10 La Liga titles. He also served as Real captain.

Quinta del Buitre

A new generation of players took over in the early 1980s. The *Quinta del Buitre* comprised five star players who all played in Real's youth system. With those five on the top club, Real won five straight La Liga titles starting in 1985–86.

FAST FACT

The other four members of the Quinta were Emilio Butragueño, Rafael Martín Vázquez, Miguel Pardeza, and José Miguel González Martín del Campo, known as Míchel. Butragueño's nickname was El Buitre or "the vulture," which led to the group's moniker.

Manuel Sanchís Hontiyuelo and his teammates celebrate after winning the Champions League final against Juventus in 1998.

Manuel Sanchís Hontiyuelo was one of the group's most important players. The defender shut down opponents. He also was one of the longest-tenured players in club history. He played in 710 games from 1983 to 2001.

The Galacticos

By the late 1990s, Real Madrid needed to make some changes. The team hadn't won a European championship in more than 30 years. And it was having little success in La Liga. So club management went after some of the biggest names from around the globe.

The moves worked, as Real won Champions League titles in 1998 and 2000. But fans wanted more, and the club was willing to spend for it. Thus, the Galacticos era began. *Galacticos* means "galaxy" in Spanish. It was meant to imply that Real's roster was filled with stars.

The club brought on creative Portuguese midfielder Luis Figo in 2000. He left archrival Barcelona to join Real, fanning the flames of that intense rivalry. Then Real added French playmaker Zinedine Zidane before the next season. The moves paid off, as Real won another Champions League title in 2002. Tied 1–1 and closing in on halftime in the final against German team Bayer Leverkusen, a ball fell to Zidane standing in the box. He struck it before it could hit the ground, and it rocketed into the net. Madrid won 2–1 on one of the defining goals in the history of Champions League competition.

But the club was not finished. It added Brazilian goal-scoring legend Ronaldo before the next season. And perhaps the biggest signing came in 2003, when the team brought English midfielder David Beckham to Madrid. He was the most popular

From left, **David Beckham, Luís Figo, Ronaldo, Zinedine Zidane, and Raúl were key figures in the Galacticos era.**

player in the world at the time. However, the group of stars failed to deliver after that 2002 Champions League title. By the time Real won its next European title in 2014, the original Galacticos were long gone.

Hometown Star

While Real Madrid added stars from around the world, one player stood out in the hearts of Real fans. Raúl played with Real from 1994 through 2010. Raúl was a hometown hero. He grew up in Madrid, but he started his youth career with Atlético. In 1992, he joined Real. He made his senior team debut on October 29, 1994. A week later, he scored a goal in the rivalry match against Atlético. Real went on to win La Liga, and a hero was born. Raúl later became Real's captain. He was known for his creativity and effort in every match.

When Raúl left the club, his 741 matches were the most played in club history. He helped set the bar high for a new generation of stars to continue the club's proud legacy.

Raúl celebrates with the Spanish flag after Real won the 2002 Champions League final.

Fly
Emirates

Iker Casillas became a legend in goal for Real.

CHAPTER 5

MODERN STARS

The *Galacticos* era reinforced Real Madrid's status as one of the top clubs in the world. But a new generation of players took the club back to European success.

For 16 years, Real was used to one man guarding its net. Iker Casillas made his senior team debut in 1999. He made 725 appearances as Real's keeper through 2015. Casillas backstopped three Champions League titles and five more La Liga titles. He is considered the best keeper in the history of Spanish soccer.

Cristiano Ronaldo's leaping ability makes him one of the best in the world at headers.

Sergio Ramos joined Real Madrid as a teenager in 2005 and quickly developed into the team's on-field leader. He carries on a tradition of fine central defenders that dates back to Sanchís. Ramos became captain in 2015. His experience and ability to make quick decisions keep Real moving.

Titanic Transfer

Cristiano Ronaldo had been tearing up the English Premier League with Manchester United. Every team in the world wanted the 24-year-old winger. But in 2009, Real Madrid paid the record price ($131 million) to get him. Some 80,000 fans greeted his arrival in Madrid before he'd even touched a ball for his new club.

The Portuguese star proved to be worth every penny. By his seventh season, he broke Raúl's team record of 323 goals. It took Raúl 16 seasons to score that many.

Ronaldo played with speed and power. Early in his career, he could torch defenders. His dribbling ability helped him create space. And his powerful leg sent goalkeepers sprawling. He helped Real to a Copa del Rey title in his second season. The next year, Real won La Liga.

FAST FACT

Galacticos-era legend Zinedine Zidane became Real Madrid's manager in 2016. He took over in the middle of the season and guided the club to the Champions League title.

As Ronaldo aged, his speed became less of a weapon, but he stayed in fine shape. His vertical leaping ability makes him one of the best in the world at headers. And he's used his head in a figurative sense as well, taking note of where he needs to be and how to get in great position to beat the keeper.

The Future Arrives

Playmaking midfielder Gareth Bale joined Real Madrid in 2013 in another record-breaking transfer. The native of Wales had an

Karim Benzema lines up a shot in a 2017 match.

immediate impact. He scored 22 goals in 44 games and Real won its first Champions League title since 2002. Bale is an expert at free kicks. His ability to bend the ball fools goalkeepers.

And he can run with the ball at his feet and still beat defenders.

Ronaldo and Bale teamed with other veterans such as French striker Karim Benzema, Croatian midfielder Luca Modrić, and Brazilian defender Marcelo to lead Real to another Champions League title in 2015–16. Ronaldo scored a tournament-best 16 goals. In a rematch of the 2014 final, Real faced rivals Atlético. Ramos put Real ahead in the 2016 final. Atlético tied it up, and the match went to penalty kicks. Ronaldo converted the game winner, giving Real its 11th Champions League title.

FAST FACT

From April 2016 through January 2017, Real did not lose a match in any competition. The unbeaten streak lasted 40 games.

Real kept it going in 2016–17 with its third European title in four years and 12th overall, beating Juventus 4–1 in the final. Ronaldo scored twice, making him the first player with goals in three Champions League finals. He also became the first player to score 100 goals in Champions League play. It was just the latest chapter in Real Madrid's lengthy story of success in Spain and throughout the world.

REAL MADRID CF
TEAM FILE

NAME: Real Madrid Club de Fútbol

YEAR FORMED: 1902

WHERE THEY PLAY: Santiago Bernabéu Stadium, Madrid, Spain

LA LIGA TITLES: 33 (most recent in 2016–17)

COPA DEL REY TITLES: 19 (most recent in 2013–14)

EUROPEAN CUP/CHAMPIONS LEAGUE TITLES: 12 (most recent in 2016–17)

KEY RECORDS

- Most appearances: Raúl, 741
- Most La Liga goals in a season: Cristiano Ronaldo, 48 in 2014–15
- Youngest player: Martin Ødegaard, 16 years, 157 days on May 23, 2015 vs. Getafe
- Most money paid for a player: $132 million for Gareth Bale in 2013

AUTHOR'S DREAM TEAM

GOALKEEPER: Iker Casillas

DEFENSE: Roberto Carlos, Sergio Ramos, Manuel Sanchís Hontiyuelo, Chendo

MIDFIELD: Francisco Gento, Zinedine Zidane, Cristiano Ronaldo

FORWARD: Alfredo Di Stefano, Ferenc Puskás, Raúl

TIMELINE

1902

The club is founded as Madrid Football Club.

1905

Madrid wins its first Copa del Rey.

1929

Madrid joins La Liga as a founding member.

1932

Madrid wins its first La Liga championship.

1936

The club shuts down for three seasons due to the Spanish Civil War.

1955

Real Madrid plays in the first European Cup and wins the title.

1960

Real wins its fifth European Cup in a row.

1990

Real wins its fifth La Liga title in a row.

1998

Real wins its first Champions League title since 1966.

2002

The original Galacticos lead Real Madrid to another Champions League title with Zinedine Zidane scoring the game-winning goal against Bayer Leverkusen in the final.

2017

Real goes back-to-back in the Champions League, beating Juventus 4–1 in the final. It's the club's third title in four years and 12th overall, the most of any team.

GLOSSARY

corner kick

A free kick from a corner of the field near the opponent's goal.

debut

First appearance.

forward

Also called a striker, a player who plays nearest the opponent's goal.

free kick

An unguarded kick awarded to a team after a foul.

knockout

A type of competition in which one loss eliminates a team.

midfielder

A player who stays mostly in the middle third of the field and links the defenders with the forwards.

relegated

Demoted from a higher league to a lower league.

rival

An opponent with whom a player or team has a fierce and ongoing competition.

stoppage time

Also called injury time, the time added at the end of each half to account for injuries and other stoppages.

FOR MORE INFORMATION

BOOKS

Hoena, Blake. *Everything Soccer.* Washington, DC: National Geographic Society, 2014.

Jökulsson, Illugi. *Real Madrid: The Most Successful Club in the World*. New York: Abbeville Press Publishers, 2014.

McDougall, Chrös. *The Best Soccer Players of All Time*. Minneapolis, MN: Abdo Publishing, 2015.

WEBSITES

To learn more about Real Madrid, visit abdobooklinks.com. These links are routinely monitored and updated to provide the most current information available.

PLACE TO VISIT

SANTIAGO BERNABÉU STADIUM

Av. Concha Espina 1, 28036, Madrid, Spain
Phone: +34 91 398 43 70
www.realmadrid.com/en/tickets/bernabeu-tour

The Bernabéu is more than the home of Real Madrid. It is history. Some of the game's greatest players have walked on its pitch. Fans get their own chance to step on that sacred ground by taking a self-guided tour. Also accessible is the Real Madrid locker room, the players' bench, the club president's box seats, and more. Fans can also visit the club museum and gift shop.

INDEX

ABOUT THE AUTHOR

Todd Kortemeier is a writer and editor from Minneapolis. A graduate of the University of Minnesota's School of Journalism and Mass Communication, he has written more than two dozen sports books for young people.